sixteen
runaway
pumpkins

WRITTEN BY **dianne ochiltree**

ILLUSTRATED BY **anne-sophie lanquetin**

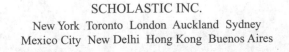

SCHOLASTIC INC.

New York Toronto London Auckland Sydney
Mexico City New Delhi Hong Kong Buenos Aires

To my Grandma Fairbanks,
who did everything with
laughter and love
—D. O.

For Elsa, Rosalie,
and their daddy, Patrice
—A.-S. L.

ISBN 0-439-79939-2

Text copyright © 2004 by Dianne Ochiltree.
Illustrations copyright © 2004 by Anne-Sophie Lanquetin.
All rights reserved. Published by Scholastic Inc.,
557 Broadway, New York, NY 10012, by arrangement
with Margaret K. McElderry Books,
Simon & Schuster Children's Publishing Division.
SCHOLASTIC and associated logos are trademarks
and/or registered trademarks of Scholastic Inc.

12 11 10 9 8 7 6 5   9 10/0

Printed in the U.S.A.   40

First Scholastic printing, September 2005

The text for this book is set in Weidemann.
The illustrations for this book
are rendered in pencils and inks.

It's harvest time in the
   pumpkin patch.

Sam tells Gramps, "Hooray!

I'll pick you lots of pumpkins.

I'll fill up my wagon today!"

Sam finds one tiny pumpkin,

then a plump one. Sam has two!

She sees two more under a vine,

playing peekaboo.

Sam dumps them into the wagon.

She counts the pumpkins there—

four of them thump-bump together.

There's plenty of room to spare!

She plunks four chunky pumpkins

next to the other four.

Eight pumpkins thunk-clunk together.

Can Sam *double* her pumpkin score?

Sam stacks eight lumpy pumpkins

on the eight-pumpkin clump inside.

Sixteen pumpkins slam-jam together.

It's one jiggly, wiggly ride!

The wagon wobbles. The wagon tips.

Pumpkins slip out from behind.

"Look out!" Sam shouts as each pumpkin becomes

the hill-rolling, bowling-ball kind.

Now, *whoosh!* The pumpkins pick up speed.

They tumble. They rumble. They glide.

They're on a roll, out of control,

on a stump-bumping, ditch-jumping slide!

Eight pumpkins skate past Gramps' garden gate.

Four dash through the open front door.

Sam runs after runaway pumpkins

that skid on Gramps' clean kitchen floor.

Gramps winks at Sam. "Don't worry," he says,

"about a cracked pumpkin or two."

He hands Sam a spoon and an old flannel shirt.

"I know just what we can do!"

Pots and pans rattle.

Egg beaters fly!

In double time Sam helps

bake pie after pie.

Sam's family comes to the table.

Forks are raised with a happy sigh.

Then Sam and her kin dig in with a grin.

They ALL feast on Sam's pumpkin pie!